USBORNE

How your body works

Judy Hindley
Assisted by Christopher Rawson

Illustrated by Colin King

Medical consultants: Susan Jenkins, MRCP, DCH and Dr. Karen Aucott
Educational consultant: Paula Varrow

Edited by Louie Stowell and Sam Lake

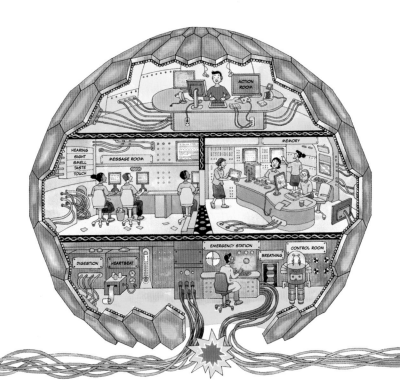

Contents

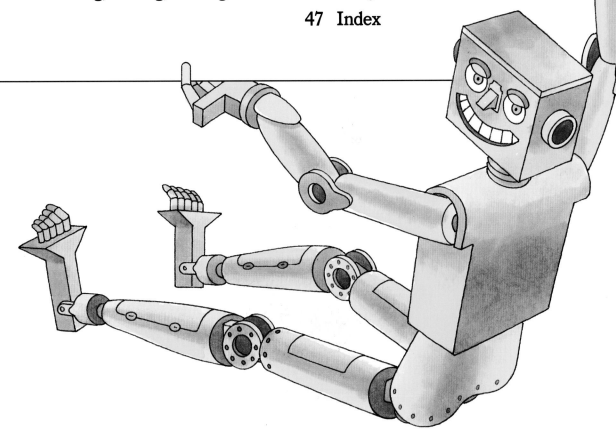

About this book

Your body is like a wonderful machine that can
do lots of different jobs all at once. This book uses lots of separate
made-up machines to show you how it does some of its most important tasks.

But no scientist has ever been able to make a single machine as neat and
light as your body, or one that can do even half the things your body does.
And no machine can have new ideas, or make jokes, or
change its mind — or make babies. At least, not yet.

Eating machine

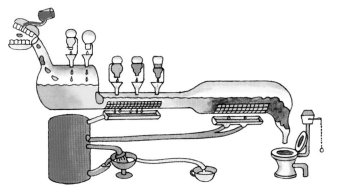

The eating machine on pages 4–5
shows what your body does to food
after you swallow it.

Breathing machine

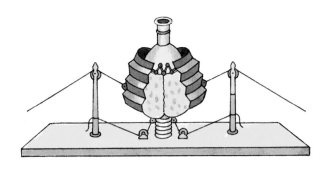

The breathing machine on pages 12–13
shows how your ribs work together with a
special muscle that helps you to breathe.

Teeth and tongue machine

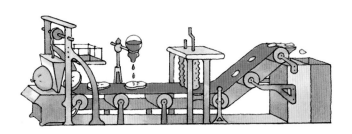

The teeth and tongue machine on
pages 6–7 shows how your mouth
chews and mushes up food.

Moving machine

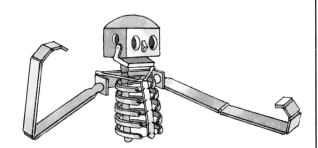

The moving machine on pages 28–31
shows how your muscles and bones work
together to move your body.

An eating machine

This apple is about to go on a trip through the eating machine.

Special juices are made by your stomach. They start changing the food into the very tiny pieces that your body can use.

Other juices in your small intestine help to change the food into tiny pieces.

Saliva (spit)

Teeth

Digestive juices

Food pipe

Digestive juices

Your teeth grind up food and mix it with saliva, so it can slide down to your stomach.

Stomach

Small intestine

In your stomach, the food becomes a wet, thin soup. A gate at the bottom of your stomach lets the soup out slowly.

Useful pieces

Inside you

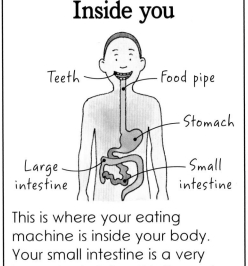

Teeth — Food pipe

Stomach

Large intestine — Small intestine

This is where your eating machine is inside your body. Your small intestine is a very long wiggly tube. It is the red bit here. Your large intestine is fatter. Here it is shown in blue.

Blood machine

The useful food pieces move around your body in your blood stream.

The useful pieces of food are taken out here. They are so tiny that they can slip through the sides of the intestine.

Used blood

Clean blood

Kidneys

What's the eating machine for?

The eating machine chops and churns food to break it up into tiny pieces.

The breaking up of food is called digestion. Special juices, called digestive juices, help to change the food into smaller parts.

The machine then sorts the useful parts of food from the useless waste. The useful parts enter your blood. The waste is sent out of your body.

Blood flows around your body a bit like a river. This flow of blood, called the blood stream, carries the useful parts of food to where they're needed.

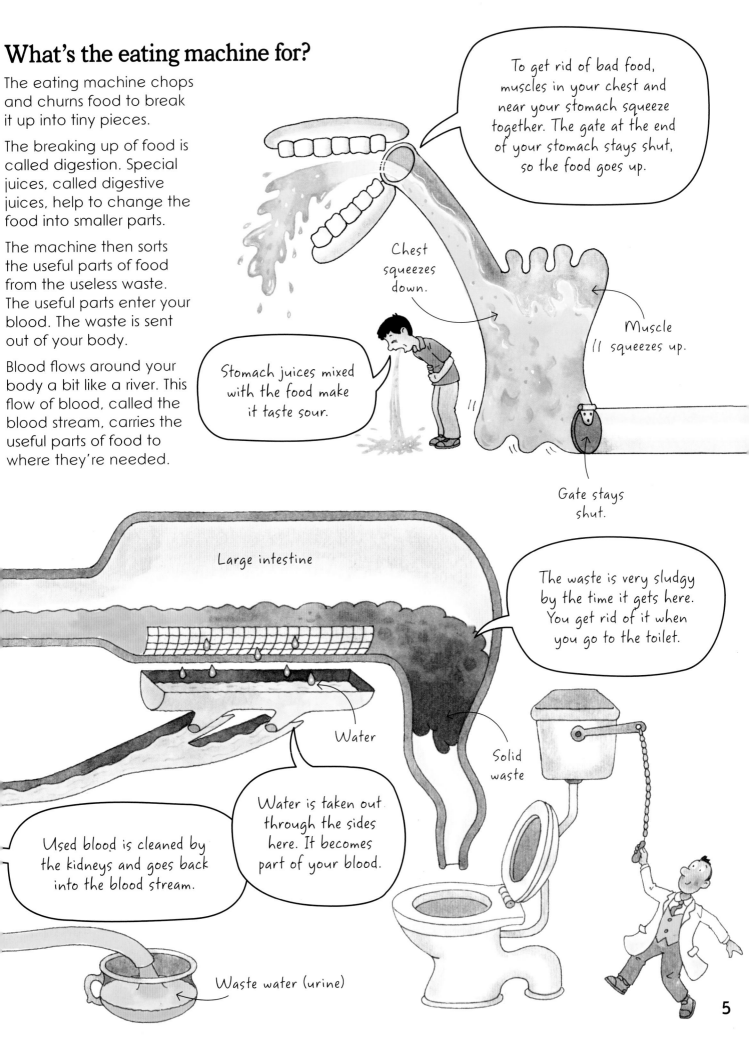

To get rid of bad food, muscles in your chest and near your stomach squeeze together. The gate at the end of your stomach stays shut, so the food goes up.

Chest squeezes down.

Stomach juices mixed with the food make it taste sour.

Muscle squeezes up.

Gate stays shut.

Large intestine

The waste is very sludgy by the time it gets here. You get rid of it when you go to the toilet.

Water

Solid waste

Used blood is cleaned by the kidneys and goes back into the blood stream.

Water is taken out through the sides here. It becomes part of your blood.

Waste water (urine)

A teeth and tongue machine

This machine gets food ready to be swallowed. That's the job your real teeth and tongue do. It has a chopper and some grinding wheels. You have special teeth for chopping and other teeth for grinding.

Saliva helps the food to slide around your mouth and between your teeth.

Chopper

Your front teeth have sharp edges to chop off bites.

Tongue

Saliva (spit)

Your tongue carries food to your grinders. It takes the mashed-up bites to the back of your throat when you swallow.

What makes teeth go bad?

Sticky liquid

Liquid from chewed food sticks to teeth. You can't see it, but it will feel sticky.

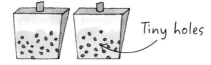

Tiny holes

If the stickiness stays, it makes holes in teeth. Germs in the air make the holes deeper.

Sensitive part

When they reach the sensitive part inside your teeth, they hurt.

How are teeth mended?

Germs live in holes in bad teeth. Dentists drill out the bad parts.

The outside of teeth cannot grow back. Dentists fill the holes to keep germs out.

What are fangs for?

Fangs are the pointed teeth next to the choppers. Some animals use them to grip prey.

A trap door at the back of your throat closes your windpipe when you swallow. You use your windpipe to breathe, so this stops you from choking.

Trap door

Tongue

Grinders

Windpipe

Food pipe

Your grinders need careful cleaning. Food often sticks between the bumps.

Your back teeth are bumpy. They work in pairs, grinding food between the bumps.

In your mouth

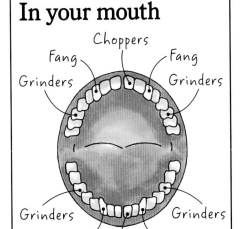

Choppers

Fang

Fang

Grinders

Grinders

Grinders

Grinders

Fang

Fang

Choppers

Teeth come in lots of different shapes to bite, chew and grind your food.

After your baby teeth fall out, you'll grow 32 big teeth.

Tongues and tasting

Salty ham

Sweet ice cream

Spots on your tongue sense different tastes. These spots are called taste buds. They send messages to your brain.

There are patches of different kinds of taste buds on your tongue. There are lots of sweet-tasters on the tip.

Sour lemon

Bitter orange peel

Your nose senses many food tastes. If you hold your nose and eat, you can only taste sweet, sour, salt and bitter.

Bitter-tasters are near the back of your tongue. Often you don't notice a bitter taste until you are ready to swallow.

What is blood?

When you prick your finger, red stuff comes out. That is blood. Most of your blood is a clear liquid called plasma. The redness comes from tiny things inside it called red blood cells.

Your entire body is made up of many different types of cells. Cells need food and a special gas called oxygen to work. Your blood stream brings those things to all the cells in your body.

Red blood cells bring oxygen from the lungs to the body cells. They take away the waste gas made by body cells as they work.

These fighting white cells kill germs that get into your body. They are bigger than red cells but you don't have so many of them.

WHITE BLOOD CELLS

OUT   IN   OUT

Oxygen   Waste gas

RED BLOOD CELLS

Plasma

Germs

How blood gets oxygen...

The air you breathe in carries oxygen. Red blood cells bring waste gas to your lungs and exchange it for oxygen.

The air you breathe out takes away the waste gas. The red blood cells carry oxygen around the body.

water...

Lots of water goes into your blood through the eating machinery. More than half of your blood is water.

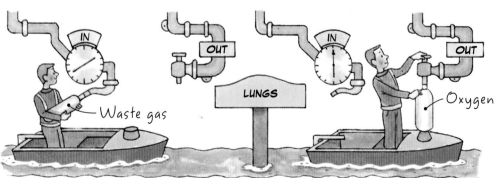

IN
Waste gas
OUT
LUNGS
IN
OUT
Oxygen

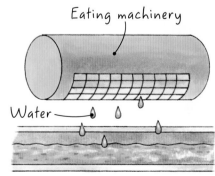

Eating machinery

Water

Group of body cells

The blood takes away any rubbish made by the cells. It's cleaned as it goes through your kidneys. Pages 4-5 show more about this.

IN OUT

BODY CELL

What blood looks like

Cells are so small that you need a very strong microscope to see them. Under a microscope, a drop of blood looks like this.

Plasma

White blood cell

Red blood cells

Waste

BODY CELL

Food

OUT IN

Plasma

Pieces of food are carried by your blood stream. The body cells pick up what they need as the blood flows past.

Waste gas

These red blood cells are carrying waste gas. They will exchange it for oxygen in your lungs and then come back.

...and food

Your blood carries bits of food from your eating machinery to your liver. Your liver sorts the food.

Your liver has to change some of the food to prepare it for your body. It stores some bits.

It sends the rest back into your blood. Your blood carries food from your liver to where your body needs it.

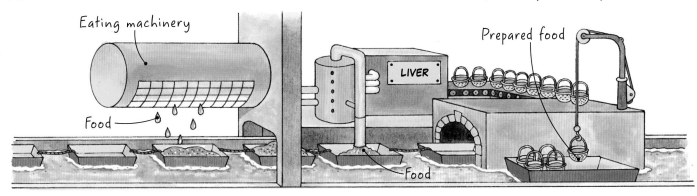

Eating machinery

Food

LIVER

Prepared food

Food

How blood goes around

Your blood stream has many tiny branches. These join up so that the blood goes around and around your body.

Your heart is a pump that keeps blood flowing around. It squeezes out blood like a squeezy bottle. It sends blood to your lungs to get rid of waste gas and to pick up oxygen. It sends blood around your body to take oxygen to all the cells.

Your blood goes through rubbery pipes called blood vessels. Page 44 shows where your main blood vessels are.

A message from your brain makes your heart squeeze. This pumps blood out and sucks it in through different tubes. Tiny gates open and shut in your heart while this happens.

How your heart works

The top squeezes...

Then the bottom squeezes...

Your heart is a muscle with four tubes, like this. The tubes are big blood vessels. The picture below shows where each of them leads. Page 45 shows what muscles are made of.

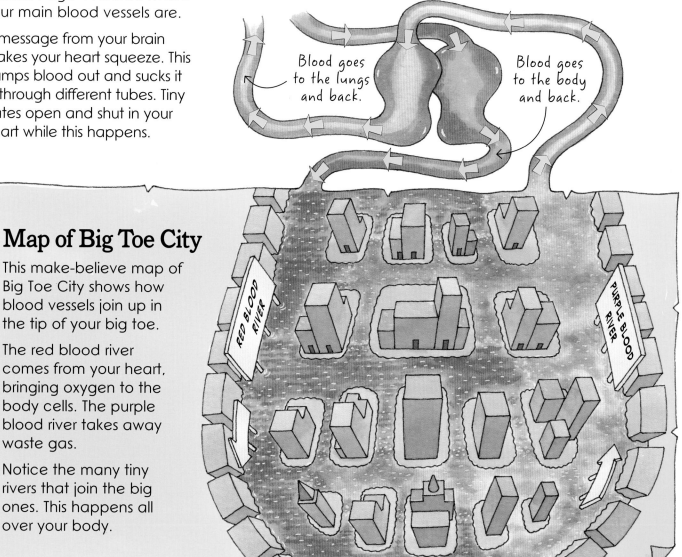

Blood goes to the lungs and back.

Blood goes to the body and back.

Map of Big Toe City

This make-believe map of Big Toe City shows how blood vessels join up in the tip of your big toe.

The red blood river comes from your heart, bringing oxygen to the body cells. The purple blood river takes away waste gas.

Notice the many tiny rivers that join the big ones. This happens all over your body.

RED BLOOD RIVER

PURPLE BLOOD RIVER

What makes your heart beat fast?

Your body has to make lots of energy when you run or play sports. Without energy you would be very tired.

Your heart has to pump very hard and fast. It has to get lots of blood up to your lungs, to get the oxygen your body needs to make energy.

Put your hand on your chest like this when you've been running. Feel how fast your heart is beating. You breathe more quickly too.

Can blood run backwards?

There are many tiny gates inside the blood vessels going to your heart. They only open one way. The blood can only go up — it can't go back.

How to see your tiniest blood vessels

Look in the mirror. Gently pull your lower eyelid down. Under it you will see small red lines. These are some of your tiniest blood vessels.

If you could join all your blood vessels, end to end, they would stretch all the way around the world.

How does your blood get back to your heart?

ZZZZ   Wiggle

As you move about, your muscles help move blood back to your heart. When you slow down, your blood slows down as well.

If you wiggle your toes when you stand in one spot for too long, you can keep your feet from going to sleep. Moving speeds the blood along.

Watch your blood move

The blue line on the inside of your wrist is blood. Rub your thumb up it, like this. The blood will stop. The line will turn white until the blood moves again.

How you breathe

Your lungs are like a sponge full of tiny holes. They hang in your chest, in a space made by your ribs and a special muscle called a diaphragm. When you breathe in, your chest swells up. Air fills your lungs like water in a sponge. This machine shows how it happens.

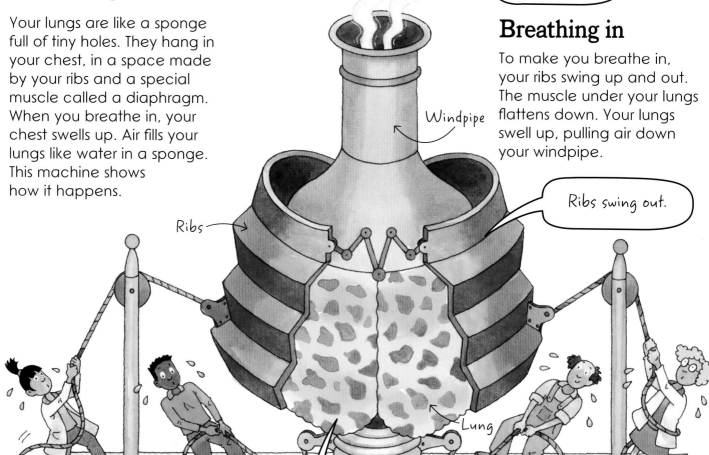

Air comes in.

Windpipe

Ribs

Lung

Ribs swing out.

Lungs swell up.

Diaphragm (muscle)

Diaphragm flattens down.

Breathing in

To make you breathe in, your ribs swing up and out. The muscle under your lungs flattens down. Your lungs swell up, pulling air down your windpipe.

A breathing machine

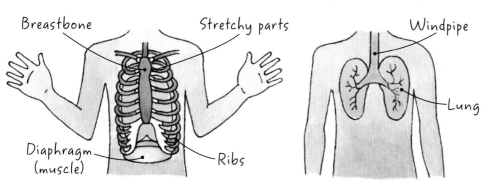

Breastbone

Stretchy parts

Diaphragm (muscle)

Ribs

Your diaphragm is shaped like an upside-down saucer. When you breathe in, it flattens and your lungs swell out.

How your lungs look

Windpipe

Lung

Your lungs are like sponges, made of tiny air sacs. Around each one is a net of blood vessels. They take oxygen from the air.

How much air?

2.5m (8ft) long

2.5m (8ft) high

2.5m (8ft) wide

Breathed out air

Lots of air goes in and out of your lungs each day. If you could trap all the air that goes out, it would nearly fill a room this big.

12

Breathing out

When you breathe out, your ribs move back. The muscle under your lungs pops up again. Air is squeezed out of the tiny air sacs in your lungs.

Feel your ribs move

Cross your arms and take a deep breath. Feel your chest swell up? Tiny muscles criss-cross between your ribs. They make your ribs swing out.

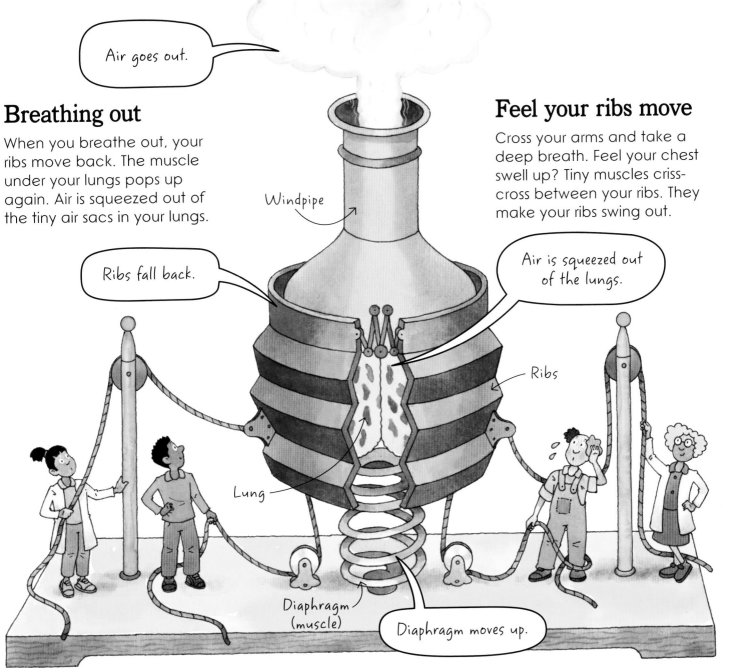

Air goes out.

Ribs fall back.

Air is squeezed out of the lungs.

Windpipe

Ribs

Lung

Diaphragm (muscle)

Diaphragm moves up.

Tummy breathing

The muscle under your lungs pushes your stomach out and in. When ladies wore tight corsets, it couldn't work, so they often fainted.

Getting more lung power

If you sing or play musical instruments such as trumpets, you need lots of puff. Learn to use the muscles under your lungs to get more lung power. To try this out, push the top of your stomach out as you breathe in. Hold your hand just under your chest, just like this lady's doing, to feel it move.

A talking machine

This machine does most of the things that you do when you talk.

You tighten your vocal cords to make them vibrate when you breathe out. This makes sound waves — special ripples in the air.

You use your teeth and tongue and mouth to turn the sound waves into words.

The shape of your mouth helps turn the sound into words.

Tongue

Sound waves

Lips

Teeth

The vibrating vocal cords make sound waves in the air.

Your lips and tongue and teeth can break up or squeeze the sound to make it into words.

Vocal cords

Your talking machine

Food pipe

Vocal cords

Lungs

Windpipe

Your vocal cords become longer when you grow up. This makes your voice sound lower. A boy's vocal cords change more than a girl's.

Windpipe

Your vocal cords are stretchy bits in your windpipe. You can tighten them. Then they vibrate as the air pushes past them.

To make a sound, you must let out air from your lungs. You use lots of air to make a loud sound.

Making words

The shape of your mouth changes to make different parts of words.

See how these people shape their mouths to make different sounds.

Watch yourself in the mirror while you talk. See how your own mouth changes shape.

Lip reading

You can sometimes work out what people are saying from the shape of their mouths.

Think how useful this might be if you were a spy!

Try it yourself. Cover your ears and watch your friends talk. See if you can work out what they are saying by reading the shape of their mouths.

Making sound waves

Blow up a balloon and let it go. The rushing-out air will make the neck flap very fast. This is called vibration. Hear the sound waves it makes?

If you put a tube in the neck like this, there will be no sound as the air rushes out. The neck can't vibrate and make sound waves.

Try stretching the neck to make high or low sounds. The tighter you stretch it, the higher the sound. Your vocal cords work in the same way.

What ears do

Your ears are machines that pick up sound waves and turn them into messages to your brain. They also send balance messages to your brain. This made-up machine can do some of the things your ears do.

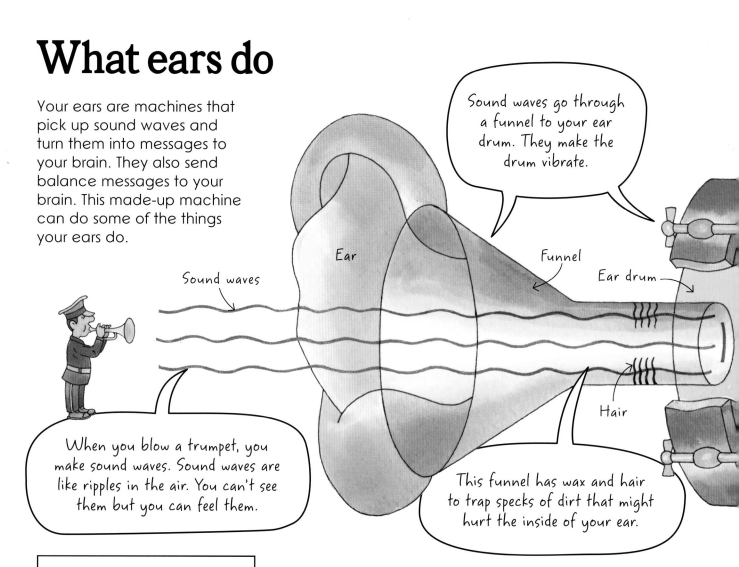

Sound waves go through a funnel to your ear drum. They make the drum vibrate.

Ear

Sound waves

Funnel

Ear drum

Hair

When you blow a trumpet, you make sound waves. Sound waves are like ripples in the air. You can't see them but you can feel them.

This funnel has wax and hair to trap specks of dirt that might hurt the inside of your ear.

Your ear machine

Your inner ear is a curled-up tube with three extra loops. The liquid in the curled-up part picks up sound waves. The extra loops are to help you keep your balance.

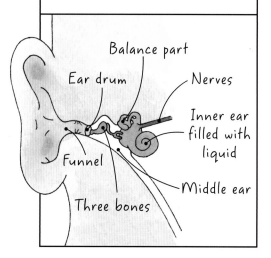

Balance part

Ear drum

Nerves

Inner ear filled with liquid

Funnel

Middle ear

Three bones

Feeling sound waves

Hold a cardboard tube against a balloon, like this, and speak into it. The sound waves will make the balloon vibrate. You can feel this with your fingertips.

Only one ear?

You need both ears to work out where sounds are coming from. Try this and see. Turn on the radio. Cover your eyes, cover up one ear, and turn around a few times. Where is the radio?

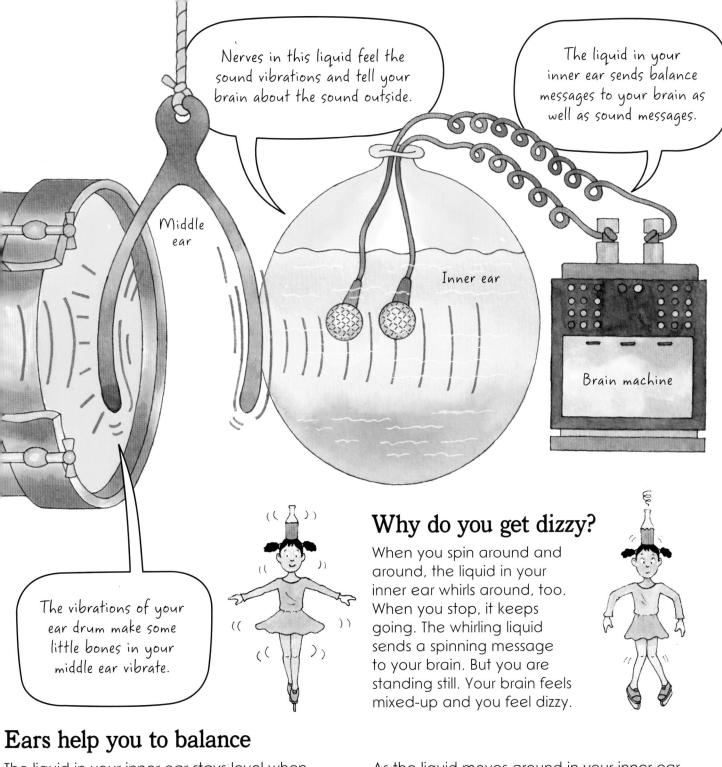

Nerves in this liquid feel the sound vibrations and tell your brain about the sound outside.

The liquid in your inner ear sends balance messages to your brain as well as sound messages.

Middle ear

Inner ear

Brain machine

The vibrations of your ear drum make some little bones in your middle ear vibrate.

Why do you get dizzy?

When you spin around and around, the liquid in your inner ear whirls around, too. When you stop, it keeps going. The whirling liquid sends a spinning message to your brain. But you are standing still. Your brain feels mixed-up and you feel dizzy.

Ears help you to balance

The liquid in your inner ear stays level when you move, like the water in this jar. See how the water sloshes around when the jar turns?

As the liquid moves around in your inner ear, nerves in the liquid tell your brain what is happening and help you keep your balance.

How eyes work

Your eyes work much like a camera. A camera takes in light rays and focuses them through different lenses to create a picture.

Each eye gathers light rays into a very tiny picture that fits on the back of your eyeball. A nerve from this spot sends the picture to your brain.

The machine on the right shows the parts of your eyes and what they do.

Light rays from the spotlight bounce off the ringmaster and make it possible to see him.

Light rays

Light rays

Light rays from the ringmaster go through this lens. The lens bends the light rays.

How your eye looks

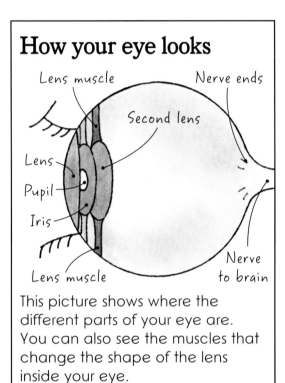

Lens muscle

Nerve ends

Second lens

Lens

Pupil

Iris

Nerve to brain

Lens muscle

This picture shows where the different parts of your eye are. You can also see the muscles that change the shape of the lens inside your eye.

What a lens does

A magnifying glass is a lens. You can make it bend light rays into an upside-down picture. Try this.

Hold a magnifying glass between a torch and some white paper. Move the glass backwards and forwards until you see a clear pattern of light on the paper. You may have to move the paper.

Now hold your thumb over the torch at the top, like this. Where is your thumb in the pattern on the paper?

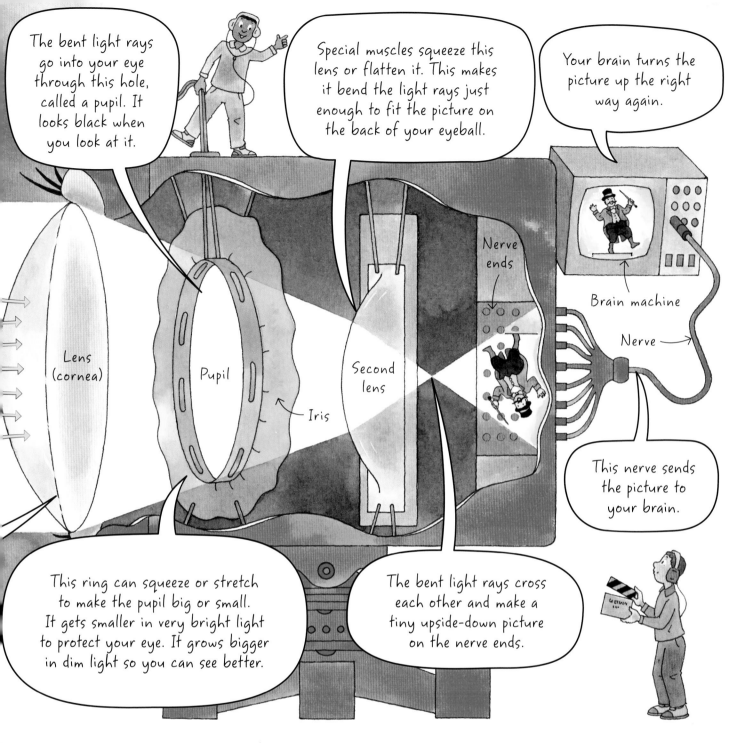

The bent light rays go into your eye through this hole, called a pupil. It looks black when you look at it.

Special muscles squeeze this lens or flatten it. This makes it bend the light rays just enough to fit the picture on the back of your eyeball.

Your brain turns the picture up the right way again.

Nerve ends

Brain machine

Nerve

Lens (cornea)

Pupil

Iris

Second lens

This nerve sends the picture to your brain.

This ring can squeeze or stretch to make the pupil big or small. It gets smaller in very bright light to protect your eye. It grows bigger in dim light so you can see better.

The bent light rays cross each other and make a tiny upside-down picture on the nerve ends.

Watch your pupils shrink

Look in the mirror. Close your eyes nearly shut. Your pupils will get bigger.

Now open your eyes quickly. Watch carefully and you will see your pupils shrinking.

How your pupil shrinks

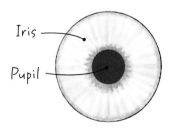

Iris

Pupil

The ring around your pupil is called the iris. If you look closely, you can see rays. These are muscles that pull your iris in and out.

How your eyes work together

Each of your eyes sees a slightly different picture of the world. Your brain puts them together.

This machine on the right shows what each eye sees when you are holding up a finger in front of your face. The brain machine shows what the eyes see when they work together.

You can try this out yourself. Hold your finger out in front of your face. Look at it with only your left eye. Then look at it with only your right eye. You will see a slightly different view of your finger each time. The view will change again if you look at your finger with both eyes.

Eyes and space

Your eyes also work together to help you tell how far away things are, or where they are in the space around you.

Pick up a pencil and close one eye. Stretch out your arm and try to touch something. Can you do it? Now open your other eye. Is it easier?

The brain puts the two pictures together.

Brain machine

The left eye can see an extra bit of the left side.

The right eye can see an extra bit of the right side.

Left eye

Right eye

What noses do

This picture shows how your nose cleans and warms the air you breathe. The air is full of germs and tiny specks of dirt. Germs are shown as little bug creatures below so you can see how they get trapped.

Gases floats away from things that have a smell. Smelly gases are shown as blue stars.

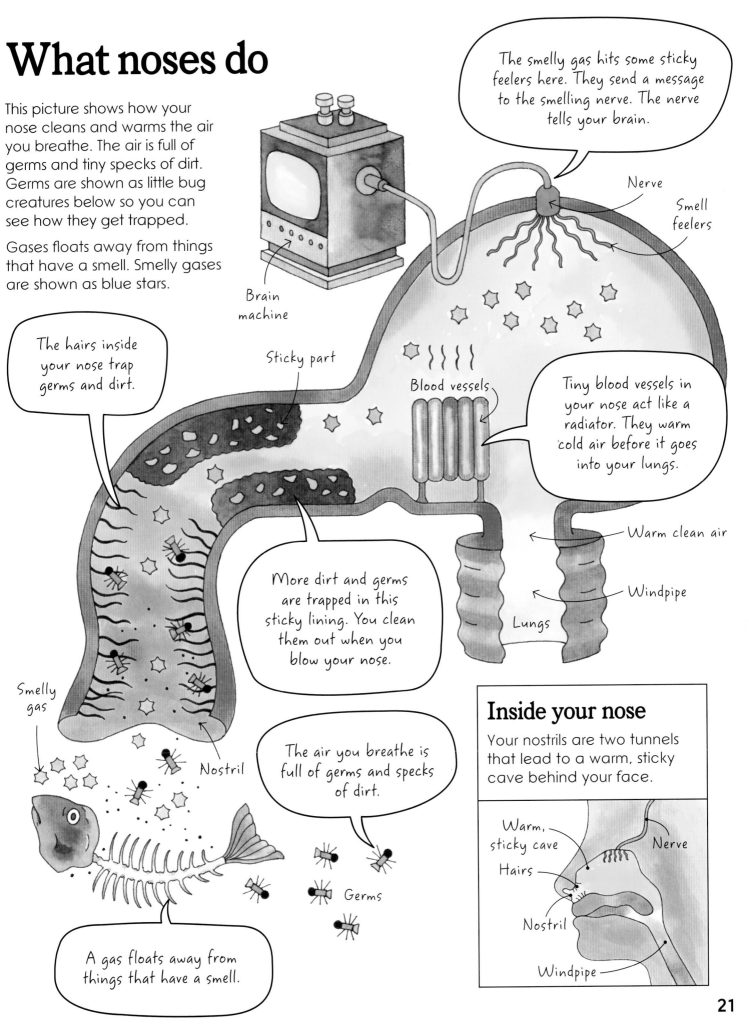

The smelly gas hits some sticky feelers here. They send a message to the smelling nerve. The nerve tells your brain.

Nerve

Smell feelers

Brain machine

Sticky part

Blood vessels

Tiny blood vessels in your nose act like a radiator. They warm cold air before it goes into your lungs.

The hairs inside your nose trap germs and dirt.

Warm clean air

Windpipe

More dirt and germs are trapped in this sticky lining. You clean them out when you blow your nose.

Lungs

Smelly gas

Nostril

The air you breathe is full of germs and specks of dirt.

Inside your nose

Your nostrils are two tunnels that lead to a warm, sticky cave behind your face.

Warm, sticky cave

Hairs

Nerve

Nostril

Windpipe

Germs

A gas floats away from things that have a smell.

21

A feeling machine

Lots of tiny nerves in your skin tell you if things are hot or cold, hard or soft, rough or smooth. You use them a lot for finding out about things.

This machine explores the world, just as your fingers do. Its feelers act like the nerves in your skin. Each kind of feeler tests for something different.

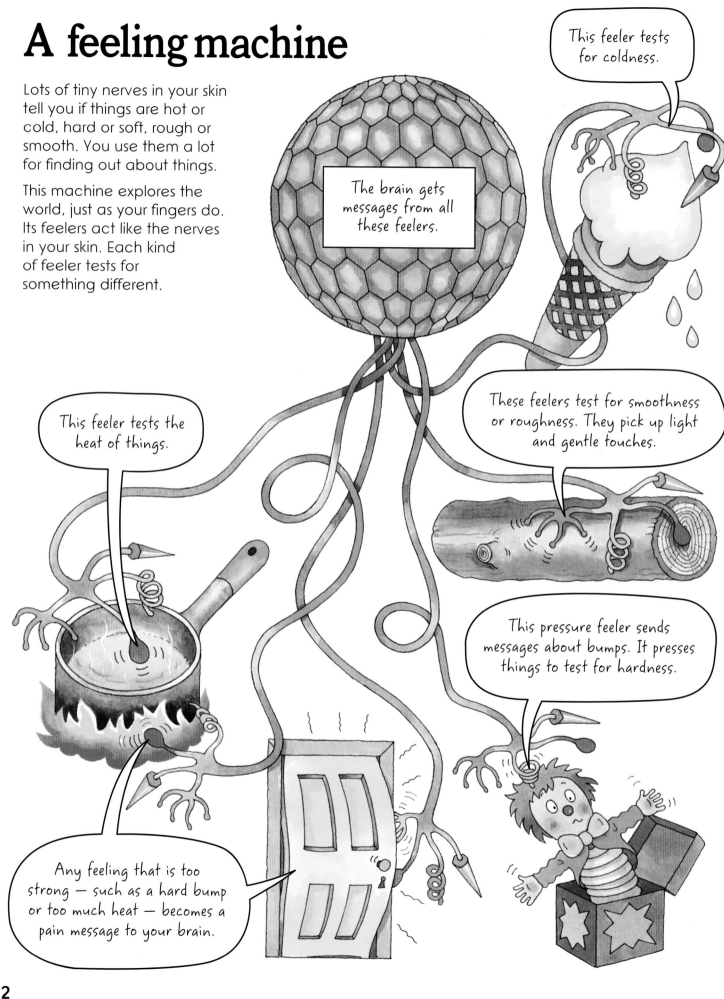

This feeler tests for coldness.

The brain gets messages from all these feelers.

This feeler tests the heat of things.

These feelers test for smoothness or roughness. They pick up light and gentle touches.

This pressure feeler sends messages about bumps. It presses things to test for hardness.

Any feeling that is too strong — such as a hard bump or too much heat — becomes a pain message to your brain.

Touching, feeling, finding out

Your brain gets feeling messages from nerves in your skin and nerves all through your body. Sometimes these messages fool your brain.

The next four pages show how your brain sorts out all the messages that come from the different parts of your body.

Mysterious pains

There's a pebble in my shoe.

I have a massive blister on my tongue.

Tiny pains on parts of your body such as your feet and tongue can feel huge. Why?

Where is it?

These places are full of feeling nerves. Your brain gets lots of pain messages — all from the same tiny spot.

Feely box trick

Cold cooked spaghetti

Fluffy cotton

Peeled grapes

For this trick you need a box with a hand hole and some things that feel funny,

Put the things inside one by one. Get your friends to stick their hands through the hole and guess what is inside.

Itchy back problems

The nerves on your back are far apart. A big space may have just one nerve. It is hard to tell where a tickle itches.

Your muscle nerves

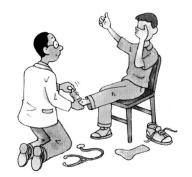

If someone lifts your toe, you can tell it is up without looking. You get messages from feeling nerves in your muscles.

Tummy ache

Nerves in your tummy tell you when something is hurting inside you. This helps people treat you when you are ill.

Back feeler trick

One? Two?

Touch someone's back with a pencil. If you then touch with two pencils close together, it may feel like only one pencil.

What happens in your brain

Your brain is a bit like mission control. It receives and sends out lots of messages and helps your body to run smoothly. This machine shows how the messages go through the main parts of your brain.

Here are your five senses

Your senses bring messages about the world around you. Your memory works out what they mean.

Hearing:
Your ears hear a noise.
Your memory says, "Car!"

Sight:
Your eyes see this.
Your memory says,
"Watch out!"

Smell:
Your nose smells this
and your memory
says, "It might
be bread!"

Taste:
Your tongue says sour.
Your memory says,
"Not ripe!"

Touch:
The skin on your fingers feels bumps and hair. Your memory helps you work out who it is.

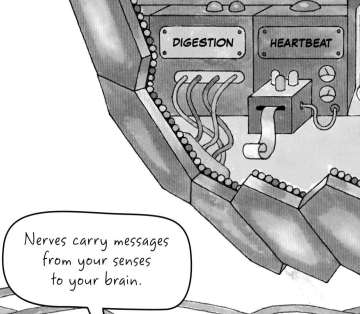

This part gets important news from your senses and helps your brain work out what to do about the news.

HEARING
SIGHT
SMELL
TASTE
TOUCH

MESSAGE ROOM

This part gets lots of messages from your senses. It checks with your memory to help decide what they mean.

DIGESTION   HEARTBEAT

Nerves carry messages from your senses to your brain.

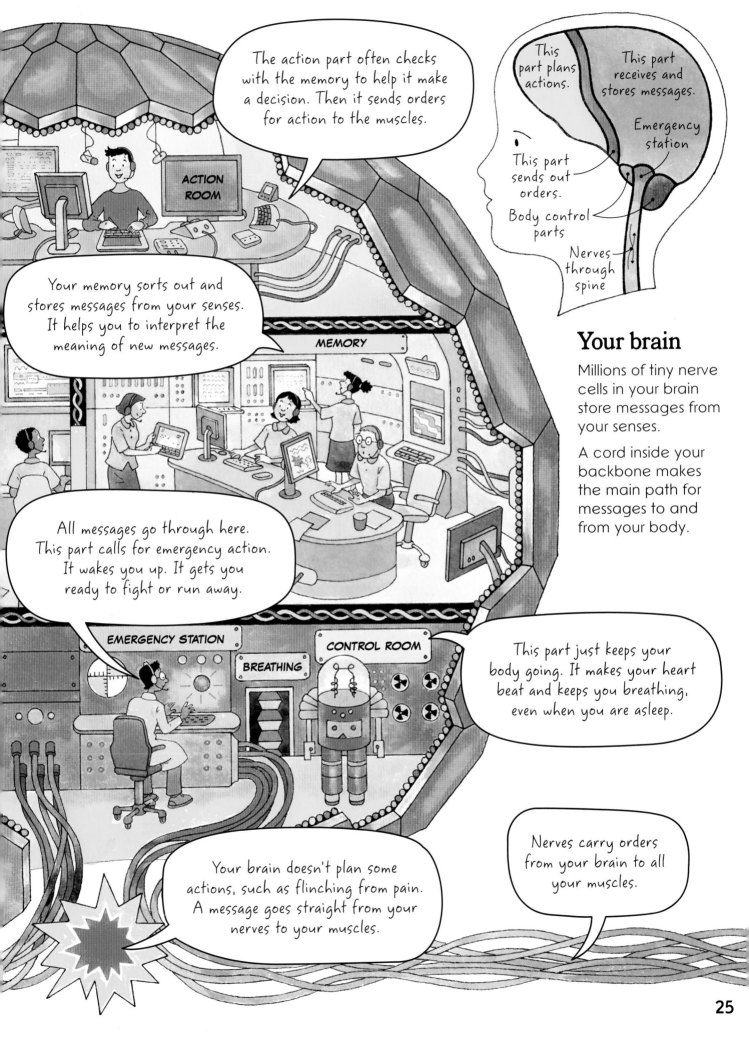

Your brain

Millions of tiny nerve cells in your brain store messages from your senses.

A cord inside your backbone makes the main path for messages to and from your body.

25

Your brain in action

This is you.

You are sleeping soundly in a quiet room. Suddenly, there's a scuffle at the window.

You open your eyes and see a strange, dark shape. You panic and reach for the lamp.

This is what's happening inside your brain.

Most of the brain is resting, but the control room is always busy and the emergency station is always ready for action.

Now that you are awake, your brain can find out more about the strange noise. The action part can get the body's muscles going.

Oh, it's only the owl that lives in the tree outside. He gives a hoot before he flies away.

You turn off the light and go back to sleeping soundly again.

Here the brain is using messages from many senses to work out what's happening. It uses memories, too.

Emergency over. Most of the brain shuts down. The emergency station will take over now, to watch over the body while it sleeps.

How bones fit together

The places where your bones link up are called joints. This made-up skeleton shows how your main joints work. This skeleton wouldn't work as well as yours. Its metal pieces would be hard to move. Real bone is light. It is full of tiny holes, like honeycomb.

You use your knee and elbow joints a lot. Try going stiff-legged and stiff-armed for half an hour. Can you eat? Can you throw a ball? Can you run? Or climb stairs?

Many little joints in your feet and ankles move when you run. Try to run on your heels and feel the difference.

This is your skeleton. Muscles join these sticking-out bits. Pads of gristle, called cartilage, make cushions between each two bones.

Elbow joint

Parts that stick out on your backbone

Knee joint

Oil

The little bones in your ankles and wrists let you make small, quick movements. The ends of the bones slide across each other.

Your body makes a special liquid that oils your joints. Otherwise you might creak.

Ligaments

Special covers help to hold joints together and keep in the oily liquid.

Tough straps called ligaments hold the joints in place.

Special cover

Your elbows and knees are special hinge joints. They can move in more ways than the joints in your fingers.

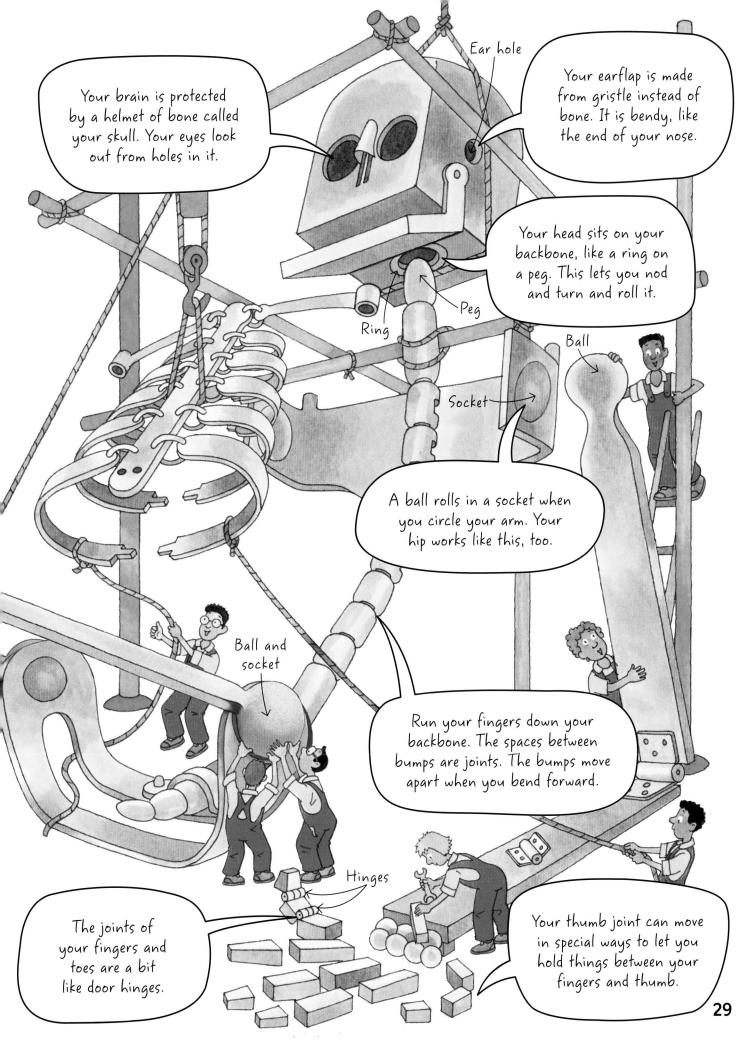

How muscles work

The springs on this metal skeleton work like muscles. Look to see how they join the moveable parts. They work these bits the way your muscles work your bones. Nerves connect these muscles to your brain. Messages from your brain make them work. Your brain can send many messages and work many muscles at the same time. Other muscles work things inside you, such as your heart. A special part of your brain keeps these muscles going.

Muscles work in pairs

Each joint is worked by two muscles. They work in turn, like this. Hold your arm near your elbow and waggle your wrist. You can feel these muscles bulge in turn.

Bend your wrist.

Straighten your wrist.

What muscles look like

A pair of your muscles look a bit like this.

Muscles

Look for the bulge when you waggle your foot. The working muscle is up near your knee.

This big tendon carries the whole weight of your body. Feel how hard it is when you stand on one foot, like this.

Big leg tendon

Leg muscles keep you upright, like the muscles in your neck and back. Most of the time you hardly notice they are working.

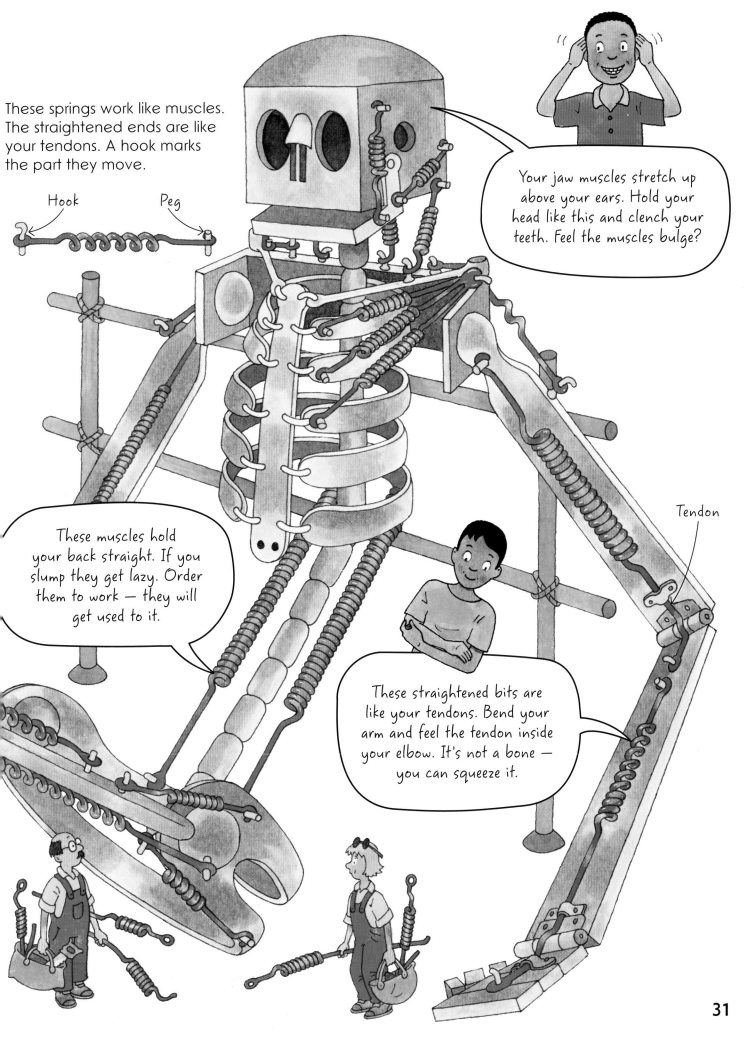

31

What skin does

All over your body is a coat of skin. You can only see the surface of it. The piece of skin on this page has been made much larger to show what happens underneath.

The skin you see (on the outside) is a layer of dead bits. This layer is dry and tough and waterproof. It protects your body from germs and from drying up.

Just under it is a second layer, where new skin is made. These new bits, fed by blood vessels in the deep layer, die as they get pushed up to the surface.

Your surface skin is dead. Every time you touch something with your fingers, you rub off a few tiny cells. New cells are pushed up to take their place.

Sometimes the pigment cells are bunched up here and there. This makes freckles.

A material called pigment gives your skin its shade. It is made in special cells in the growing layer.

Pores are tiny holes in your surface skin. You can see them with a very strong magnifying glass.

Hair

Dead skin cells

Freckle

Dead skin

Growing skin

Deep skin

New skin

Blood vessels

Hair root

Pigment cells

Hair muscle

Pore

Oil is made here. It is squeezed out when the hair muscle tightens up. It oils your hair and skin.

Your hair is dead. The hair cells are pushed up from a live root in the deep layer. Every few years the root has a rest and the hair falls out. Later the root grows a new hair.

These little tubes take water and salt from your body and make sweat. Sweat goes out through the pores in your skin.

If you had no skin?

Your body is made mostly of water. If you had no skin, the sun and air would dry you up like a prune.

Skin is waterproof

Your skin makes oil which helps to keep it waterproof. Water does not soak into your skin. You can rub it off.

Why should you wash?

Dirt and dust from the air stick to the oil made by your skin. You use soap and warm water to get the dirty oil off.

When it is hot and sunny

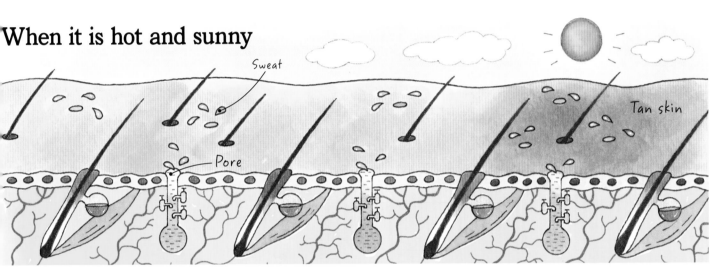

When you are hot, the sweat glands make more sweat. The sweat goes out through pores. As it dries it cools your skin.

Your blood takes heat from your body. When you are hot, more blood moves near the skin's surface. The air cools it.

Some of the sun's rays are bad for you. In strong sunlight, pigment cells go darker, to protect you from harmful rays.

When it is cold

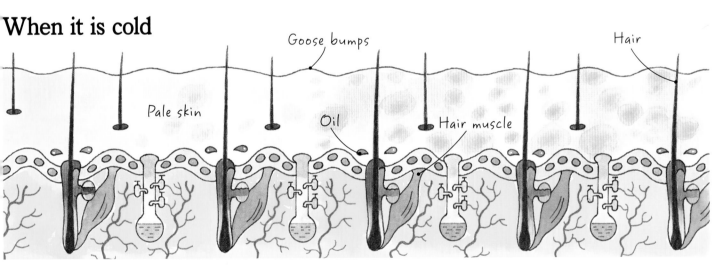

When it is cold your blood vessels squeeze down in your skin to keep warm. This makes you look paler.

Cold makes your hair muscles tighten and get short and fat. This squeezes out oil and also makes goose bumps.

When a hair muscle tightens, it makes your hair stand up. On furry animals, hair traps in air to keep them warm.

How bodies fight germs

Your body is always being attacked by germs. But it is well defended, like the castle in this picture. Your skin makes a strong barrier — like the castle wall.

Germs cannot get through healthy skin. If skin is hurt, cells in the blood help to heal it and fight off the germs. They act like the warriors here.

Germs can get into your body through openings such as your mouth and your nose. But each of these is protected in some way. And there are ways you can help your body to defend itself. Look around and see.

> Tears kill germs. When you blink, tears wash your eyes.

> Your nose has sticky hairs that trap germs in the air you breathe.

> Saliva washes germs down into your stomach. Stomach juices can kill most germs.

> Your mouth is an easy place for germs to get in. Be careful what you put in it.

Germ army

Saliva (spit)

What are germs?

Germs are tiny creatures, too small to see. They make poisons. If they get into your body they make you ill.

Germs like dark, dirty places. Sun, fresh air and soapy water kill them. Good food helps your body to fight them.

Injections

If an army of strong germs attacked, you would be very ill. So the doctor shoots a few weaker germs into you.

Your ear hole has wax and hairs to trap germs.

Special white cells in your blood fight germs. Different kinds do different jobs. Some of them corner the germs and others kill them.

Your blood is always moving around your body. When germs attack, your blood carries messages for help. Then lots of fighting white cells come.

Red blood cells

White blood cells

Repair cells make a net and other cells bunch up behind it. Then blood cannot run out and germs cannot get in.

Ear hole

Cut

Sweat pores

Tiny holes called pores let out sweat. Clean sweat kills germs. But old sweat traps dirt — so wash it off.

Your blood has special repair cells. When you are cut, they make some gluey stuff that turns tiny bits in your blood into a net.

What is a scab?

Your blood cells study the weak germs to learn how to destroy the army of strong germs before they arrive.

Part of your blood makes a net when you are cut. Your blood cells bunch up behind it. This makes a blood clot.

Dried clotted blood is called a scab. A scab protects you until new skin is built. Then the scab falls off.

A healthy eating machine

This machine is sorting food into five groups. You need to eat the right amount of food from each group to keep your body healthy. The wheel on the right shows which foods you need to eat more of and which ones you should eat in smaller amounts.

Tomatoes, oranges and lemons help to fight germs.

It's ok to eat small amounts of food with lots of sugar and fat.

You need to eat about five servings of fruit and vegetables a day.

Fruit and vegetables are full of important things called vitamins, which help your body to stay healthy.

Carbohydrates include bread, pasta and rice. White types are not as good for you as the whole-grain (brown) types.

FRUIT AND VEGETABLES

CARBOHYDRATES

Wholegrain foods, such as breakfast cereals, give your body lots of energy.

How a baby starts

A baby starts when a sperm cell from a man's body joins with an egg cell in a woman's body. Men and women have special parts for making these cells and helping them to join.

A baby is a huge responsibility, so making a baby is not a good idea until you are much older. This father machine and mother machine are ready to make a baby.

Boy parts

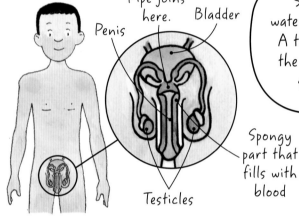

Pipe joins here.

Penis

Bladder

Testicles

Spongy part that fills with blood

A boy's testicles are his sperm tanks. They start working when he is about 14. The sperm pipes join the pipe that takes waste water from the bladder.

Extra blood pumps into the spongy walls of the penis. This makes it long and hard.

Sperm and waste water use the same pipe. A tiny gate shuts off the waste water while sperm goes out.

Brain

Blood machine

Sperm cells go out through the penis. It must get long and strong to reach inside the woman's body.

FATHER MACHINE

Blood vessel

Penis

Sperm tank

Waste water tank

The sperm tanks are called testicles. They make lots of sperm each day. They store it until all the machinery is ready to work.

How they join up

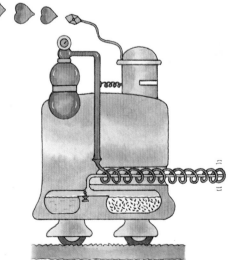

Extra blood pumped into the penis makes it stretch out.

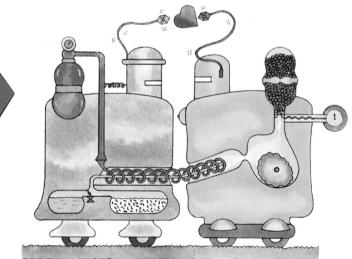

The vagina gets soft and stretchy. This makes it easy for the penis to fit in.

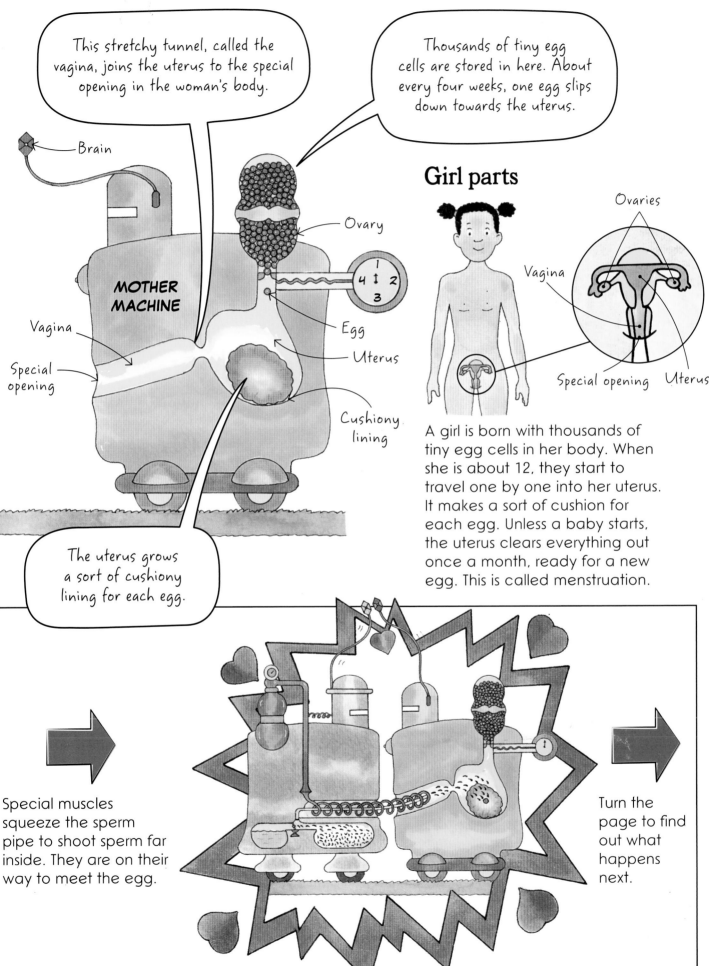

This stretchy tunnel, called the vagina, joins the uterus to the special opening in the woman's body.

Thousands of tiny egg cells are stored in here. About every four weeks, one egg slips down towards the uterus.

Brain

Ovary

MOTHER MACHINE

Vagina

Special opening

Egg

Uterus

Cushiony lining

The uterus grows a sort of cushiony lining for each egg.

Girl parts

Ovaries

Vagina

Special opening

Uterus

A girl is born with thousands of tiny egg cells in her body. When she is about 12, they start to travel one by one into her uterus. It makes a sort of cushion for each egg. Unless a baby starts, the uterus clears everything out once a month, ready for a new egg. This is called menstruation.

Special muscles squeeze the sperm pipe to shoot sperm far inside. They are on their way to meet the egg.

Turn the page to find out what happens next.

How a baby is born

These pictures show what happens as a baby grows in its mother and when it is born.

No one knows a baby has started.

The baby is just a dot inside the mother.

The baby's story

Before they start...

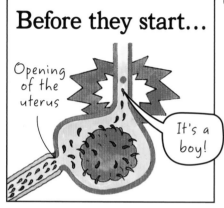

Opening of the uterus

It's a boy!

First, sperm swims up to meet the egg. It has a message that decides whether a boy or a girl is made. A sperm is much smaller than an egg.

At the beginning...

Egg

Uterus lining

The egg is joined by just one sperm. It grows by splitting into more and more cells. The growing egg nestles down into the lining of the uterus.

At one month...

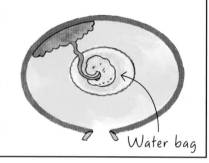

Water bag

The cluster of cells is about the size of a small bean. It has grown a water bag around itself. The baby grows inside, warm and safe.

The mother's breasts are getting bigger, ready to make milk for the baby.

At nine months...

The baby is now ready to be born. His head is down, like this. This will help when the muscles of the uterus start to push him out.

When the muscles squeeze, she knows the baby will soon be born.

At the start of birth...

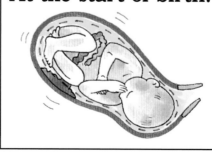

The muscles of the uterus squeeze and stretch, to make the opening wide. The baby's water bag bursts. He doesn't need it any more.

The muscles squeeze and squeeze. This is hard work.

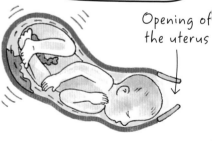

Opening of the uterus

The muscles have worked for hours now. See how wide the opening of the uterus is. The baby's head presses against it. This helps it to open.

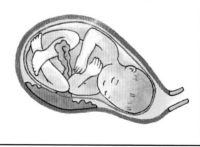

Now the mother knows a baby has started. Her uterus has kept its special lining.

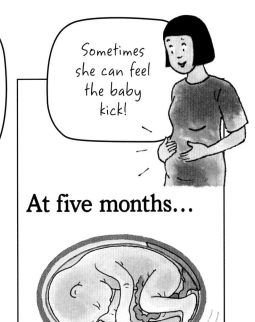

By this time she can feel a small bump where the baby is growing.

Sometimes she can feel the baby kick!

At two months...

Feeding stem

Now the baby looks a bit like this. Food and oxygen from the blood in the lining of the uterus go through a sort of feeding stem to the baby.

At four months...

The bean shape has now grown arms and legs. The cluster of cells is a complete baby. But he is still too weak to live in the outside world.

At five months...

The baby grows bigger and stronger every day. He can move about now. He even kicks sometimes. The doctor can hear his heart beating.

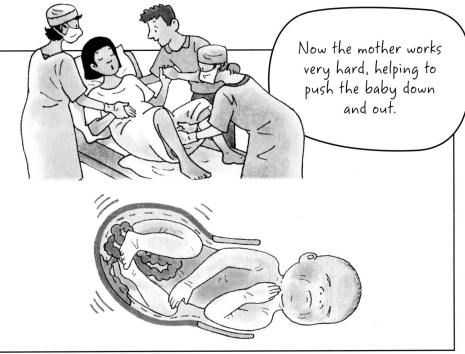

Now the mother works very hard, helping to push the baby down and out.

Now the muscles of the uterus begin to squeeze very hard. They push the baby's head right through the opening of the uterus.

Then the baby slides through the mother's vagina. This little tunnel can stretch very wide for the baby to go through. And the baby is born!

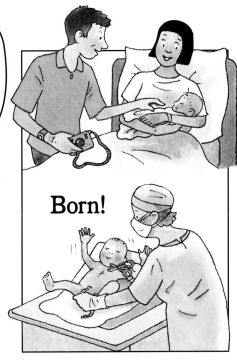

Born!

The baby's own eating and breathing machinery is now working, so the feeding stem is cut and tied. The knot becomes a belly button.

How your body fits together

The pictures on the next three pages show some of the
main parts of your body. Your breathing, eating and peeing
machinery do important work and need to be kept safe. Your
skeleton and muscles help to do this.

Your breathing machine

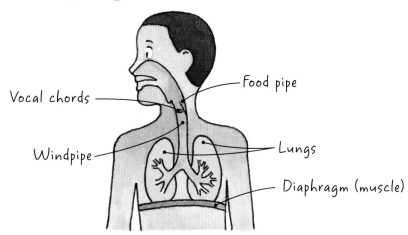

Vocal chords

Food pipe

Windpipe

Lungs

Diaphragm (muscle)

Your lungs are underneath your ribs. They connect to your
windpipe and hang above a muscle called the diaphragm.

Your skeleton

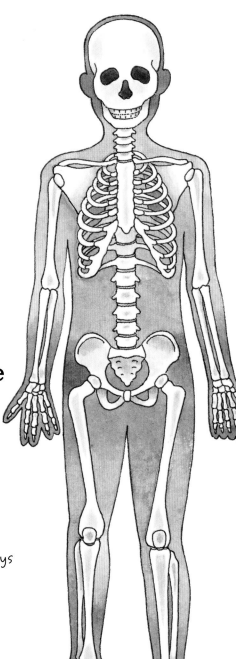

Your eating machine

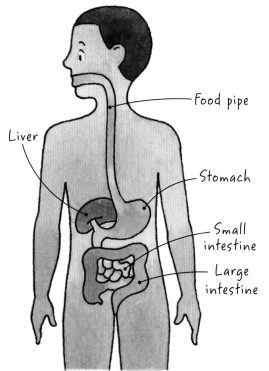

Food pipe

Liver

Stomach

Small intestine

Large intestine

Fine thready bits hold your
intestines to your backbone.
Your back and stomach
muscles help protect them.

Your peeing machine

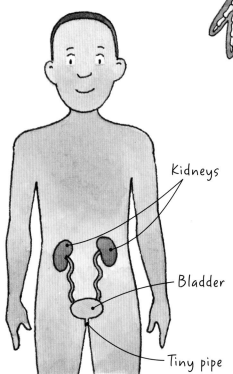

Kidneys

Bladder

Tiny pipe

Waste water stored in your
bladder goes through a tiny
pipe. A boy's pipe is longer
than a girl's.

The machinery in your body
is protected by your skeleton,
which is made up of more
than 200 bones.

Front muscles

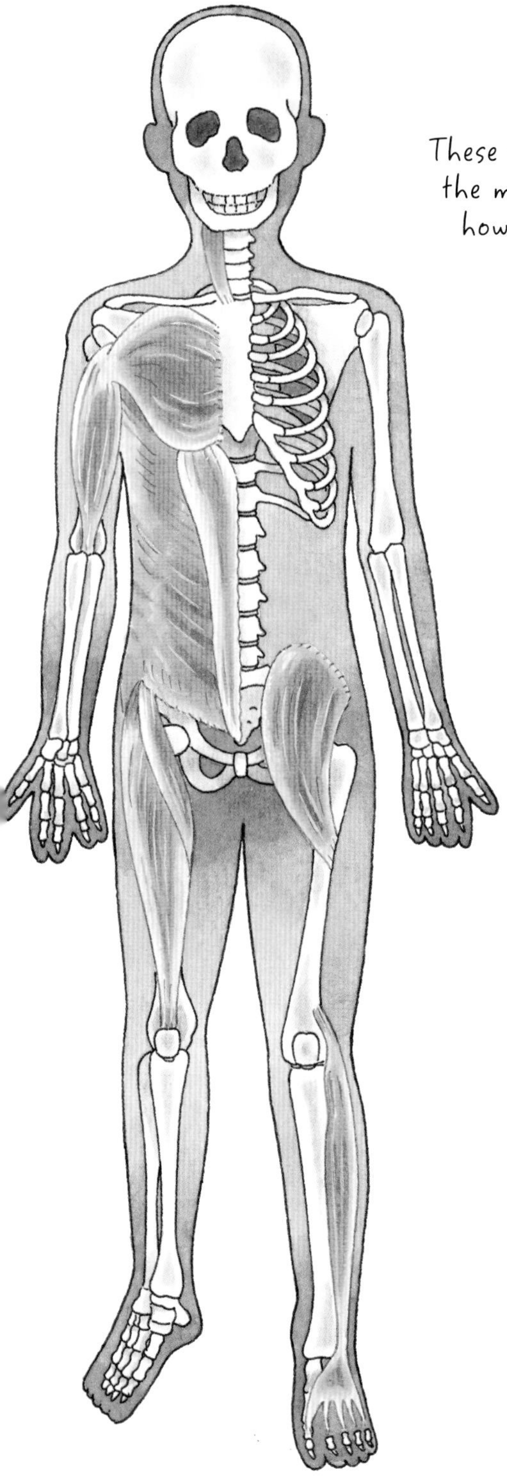

Back muscles

How muscles look

These tiny lines on the muscles show how they pull.

Layers of muscle cover your skeleton. These are some of the main muscles that join the front of your skeleton.

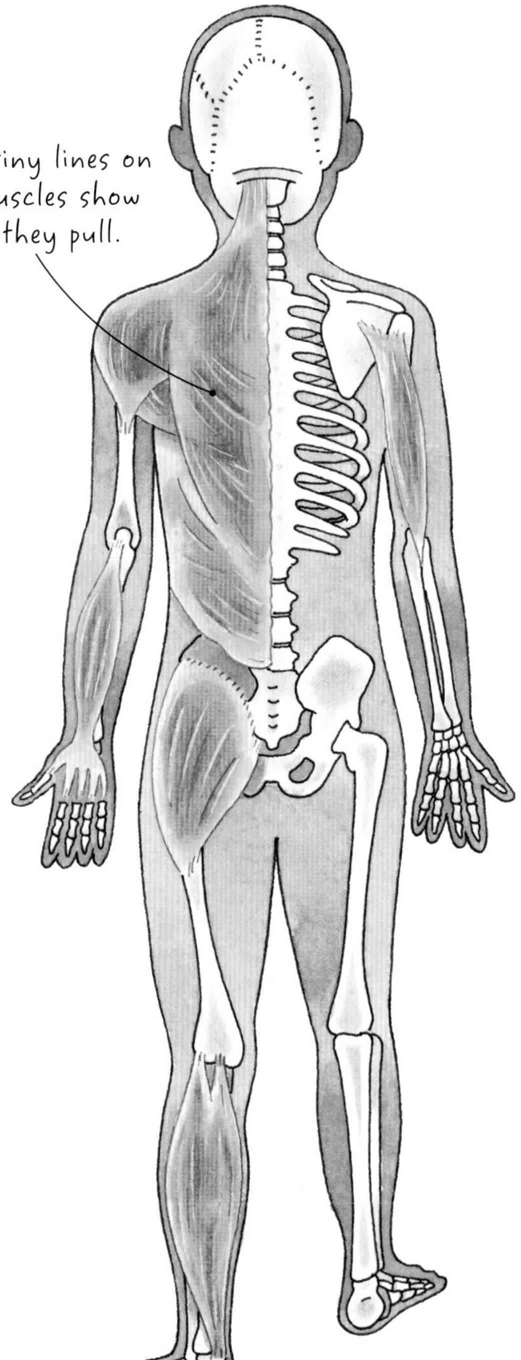

This picture shows some of the big muscles that join the back of your skeleton.

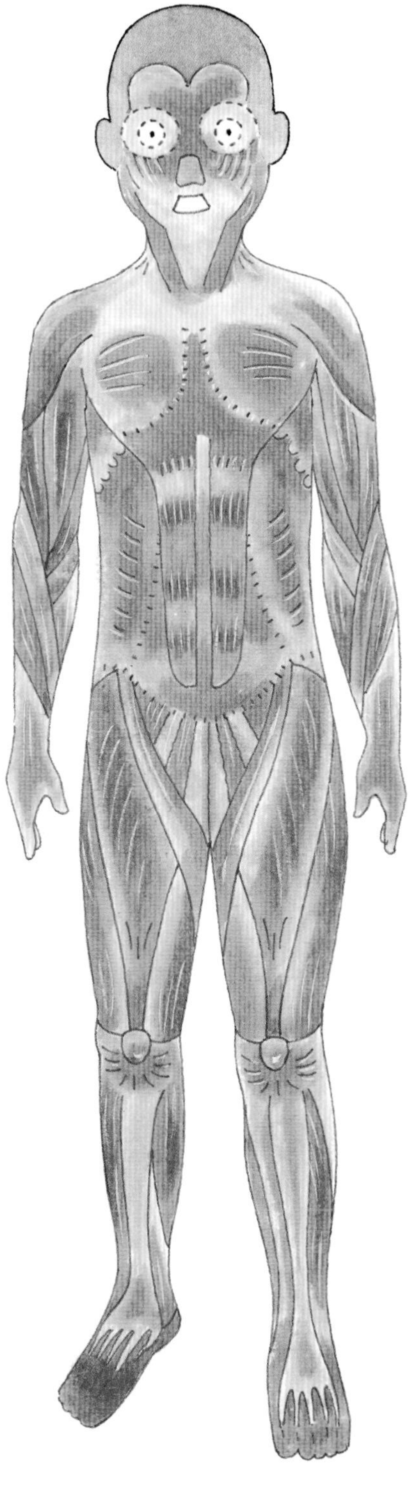

Your muscles weave together, like this, to make a fleshy envelope for your body. This is then covered by your skin.

Your main blood vessels

Your main nerves

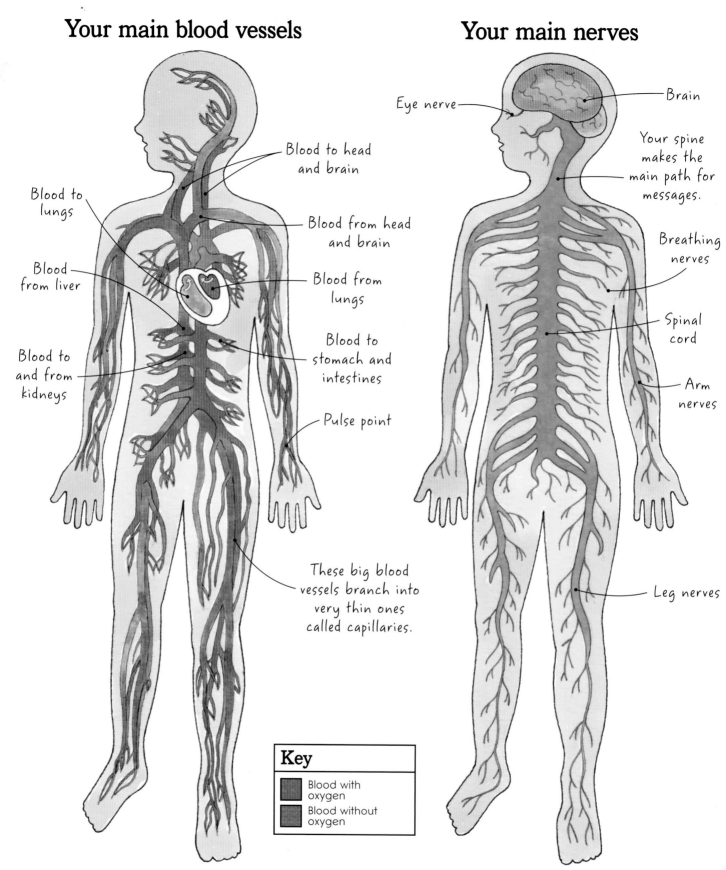

Blood to head
and brain

Blood from head
and brain

Blood to
lungs

Blood from
lungs

Blood
from liver

Blood to
stomach and
intestines

Blood to
and from
kidneys

Pulse point

These big blood
vessels branch into
very thin ones
called capillaries.

Eye nerve

Brain

Your spine
makes the
main path for
messages.

Breathing
nerves

Spinal
cord

Arm
nerves

Leg nerves

Key

■	Blood with oxygen
■	Blood without oxygen

Here, the heart looks a little bigger than it
really is, to show you how the blood goes
through it. The blood vessels leading out
of your heart are called arteries. The ones
leading back to your heart are called veins.

The main path for messages to your brain
goes right through the middle of your
backbone. The main nerves connect to it
like this. Hundreds of tiny nerves join these
big ones.

What are bodies made of?

Your body, like all living things, is made of very tiny parts called cells. You have many kinds of cell. Each does a different kind of work. Here are some of them.

How big is a cell?

Most cells are so small you would need a very strong microscope to see them.

To see how very small they are, peel off one of the layers of thick skin on an onion. Under it you will find a sort of thin tissue. This is just one cell thick. It is so thin you can see through it.

A muscle cell

This is a muscle cell. It can squeeze and stretch.

Muscle tissue

Muscle cells join into stringy bits called fibres.

A muscle

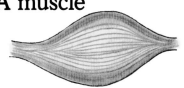

A muscle squeezes when all of the cells squeeze.

A nerve cell

The long branch-like bits pick up and carry messages.

A bundle of nerve cells

Nerve cells join together into bundles. These bundles join the main cable in your spine that goes to your brain.

Red blood cells

Blood is made of blood cells floating in a clear liquid.

Inside blood vessels

Red blood cells carry oxygen to other body cells. The liquid part of your blood carries bits of food.

Skin cells

Only the bottom layer of cells is alive.

A cell grows like this

This picture shows how a new cell is made. The growing skin cell is shown in red. It swells until it breaks into two cells.

Body words

Eating words

Abdomen The part of your body under your chest where your stomach and intestines are found.

Anus The hole where solid waste goes out of your body.

Bladder The bag that stores waste water.

Carbohydrates Foods such as bread, pasta and potatoes.

Epiglottis A flap of cartilage behind your tongue that stops food going down your windpipe.

Fats Foods such as olive oil, nuts and avocados.

Oesophagus The food pipe that goes to your stomach.

Proteins Foods such as meat, eggs, beans and fish that help to build muscle.

Urine A mixture of water and waste taken from your blood by your kidneys. It is stored in your bladder until it goes out of your body.

Vitamins Important things in food that help your body to fight germs and stay healthy.

Breathing words

Bronchial tubes The tubes that lead from your windpipe to your lungs.

Diaphragm The sheet of muscle between your lungs and your stomach that helps you to breathe.

Larynx The part of your windpipe that holds your vocal cords.

Lungs The two air bags in your chest that you use for breathing.

Trachea Your windpipe.

Blood and heart words

Antibody A special weapon made by the blood to fight germs.

Artery A blood vessel that takes blood from your heart to elsewhere in your body.

Blood vessel A tube that carries blood.

Capillary A very thin blood vessel that brings food and oxygen to the cells and takes away waste gas.

Plasma The watery, liquid part of the blood.

Vein A blood vessel that carries blood to your heart from elsewhere in your body.

Bone, muscle and skin words

Cartilage Gristle, which is a bit like bendy bone.

Joint Where two bones link.

Pigment A material that gives your skin its shade.

Spine Your backbone.

Tendon A tough, stringy piece that connects muscle to bone.

Vertebra One of the bones that make up your backbone.

Baby-making words

Fertilization The joining of an egg and a sperm to start making a baby.

Menstruation The clearing out of the uterus each month if a baby does not start.

Ovary The part of a girl's body that stores eggs.

Ovum The egg cell in a girl's body that becomes a baby when it is fertilized.

Penis The part of a boy that lets out urine and sperm.

Placenta The cushiony lining of the uterus that brings food to an unborn baby and takes away waste.

Puberty The time when the baby-making machinery starts working in a girl or boy.

Sperm The special cells made by a boy's testicles that can fertilize a girl's egg cells.

Testicle The part of a boy's body that makes and stores sperm.

Umbilical cord The feeding tube that connects the placenta to the unborn baby.

Uterus The part of a girl where an unborn baby grows.

Vagina The passage that leads from the opening between a girl's legs to her uterus.

General words

Cell The very tiny parts all living things are made of.

Nerves Tiny threads that carry messages to and from your brain.

Organ A group of tissues that work together to do a special job. Your heart is an organ

Oxygen A special gas in the air that your body needs to live, grow and work.

System A group of organs that work together. Your heart and blood vessels together make up your blood system.

Tissue A group of cells that look and act the same, such as muscle tissue.

Index

This new edition published in 2013 by Usborne Publishing Ltd., Usborne House, 83-85 Saffron Hill, London, EC1N 8RT, England. www.usborne.com

Designed by John Jamieson, Geoff Davies, Fiona Brown and Matthew Preston